SNOOPY'S
Book of Colours

Peanuts® characters created and drawn by Charles M. Schulz

Text by Nancy Hall
Background illustrations by Art and Kim Ellis

A GOLDEN BOOK • NEW YORK

Western Publishing Company, Inc., Racine, Wisconsin 53404

Yellow

What can you find that is yellow?

A coat and umbrella
To keep off a shower,
A dress and a book,
Plus a bird and his flower.

Red

Count the things that are **red**.

The Flying Ace's scarf
Is a nice shade of red.
So's Charlie Brown's shirt,
Lucy's card, and my bed.

Brown

How many **brown** things
do you see in this picture?

Brown is the colour
Of a football that's new,
Tree bark, ice-cream cones,
And Linus's shoe.

Orange

Do you see many things that are orange?

Peppermint Patty's
And Marcie's shirts match
Charlie Brown's ball and
The Great Pumpkin Patch.

Blue

What things can you find that are **blue**?

Linus's shirt and
My dog dish are blue,
The pillow and golf bag,
The summer sky, too.

Pink

Now count the pink things.

Charlie Brown likes ice cream—
Strawberry, I suppose.
Lucy found pink flowers
To go with Sally's clothes.

Purple

Do you see any **purple** things?

I see some pom-poms,
All purple and white;
A headband, a balloon,
And Charlie Brown's kite.

Black

What can you find that is **black**?

Musical notes and
Pianos are black,
Plus bowling balls, phones,
Lucy's hat and her sack.

Green

How many **green** things can you see?

Green are the leaves,
The cactus, the ball,
The Flying Ace helmet—
Goggles and all.

Rainbow

Put the colours together
and what do you have?